For Miriam

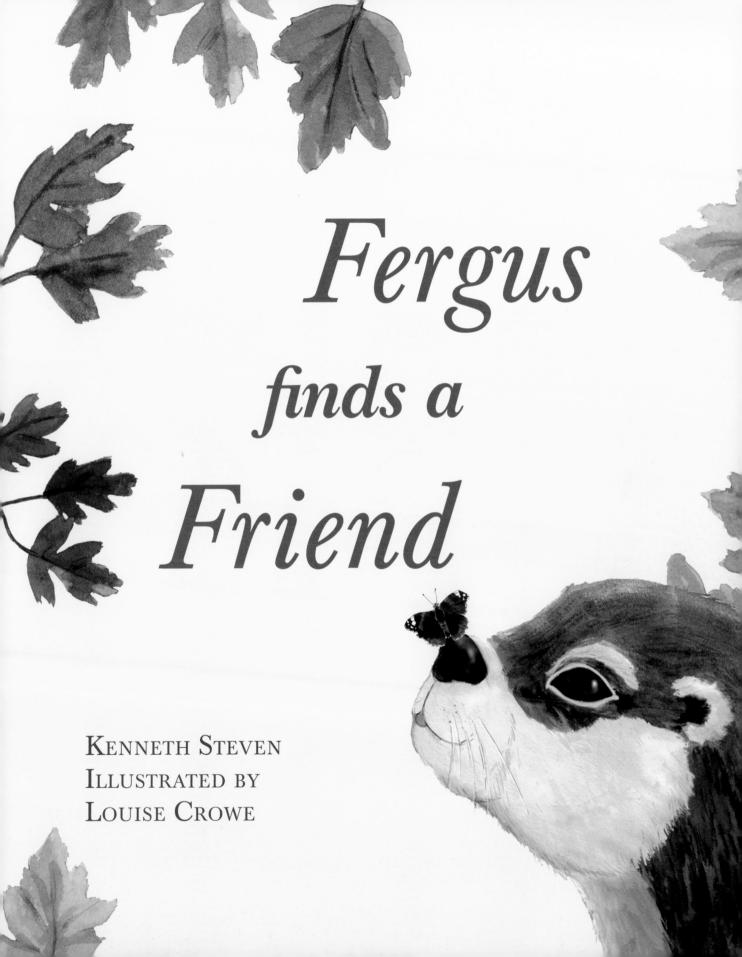

Fergus
finds a
Friend

KENNETH STEVEN
ILLUSTRATED BY
LOUISE CROWE

Fergus was leaving home. He'd gone on many journeys with his mother before, but now it was time for the young otter to leave home for good.

His mother and brothers popped their heads out of the holt to say goodbye. Fergus climbed down the bank to the river and turned round one last time to his family. He felt excited and frightened at the same time. This was the beginning of his very own adventure.

Fergus followed the stones by the river. It was still early morning and the whole world seemed fast asleep.

The newborn lambs lay in the fields beside their mothers, looking clean and white as snow.

The otter stopped in his tracks. A robin was watching Fergus curiously, its red tummy all fluffed-out and handsome. It had never seen an otter before and Fergus had never seen a robin before.

All of a sudden a butterfly fluttered right in front of his nose. Fergus forgot about the robin as he tried to follow the butterfly. He wished that he could fly in the air too!

But the butterfly flew higher and higher into the trees until it had disappeared completely. The young otter wished it had stayed longer to play.

Soon the river ran down into a black pool.

Fergus came to the edge and there, to his horror, he saw another otter looking up at him! He froze. What should he do?

Very slowly he raised one paw. So did the other otter.

Then he raised the other paw. So did the other otter.

Then Fergus realised it wasn't another otter at all.

He was looking at his own reflection.

SPLAASHH!

Fergus dived deep into the pool. He circled and paddled and swam until he remembered his journey, then clambered out onto the bank once more.

Just then the morning sun came out for the first time. Fergus looked up and sneezed.

It was lovely and warm.

Fergus climbed up the riverbank to the sunny fields. He felt excited. This was the beginning of his very own adventure!

Aaa-choo!

A bark. Fergus froze. Three huge dogs came bounding out of the wood towards the field.

The otter was off down the path like a shot. The dogs were heading straight for him. What was he going to do?

Ahead of him was a rock – if only he could make it as far as that …

Fergus plunged over the side of the rock and down a steep mudslide all the way to the river's edge.

Slither slide squelch!

At the bottom he turned round and looked back up. There were the three dogs, whining, their tongues hanging out like bits of hot bacon. They couldn't come any further. Fergus was safe.

When he started his journey once more, Fergus realised that this was the furthest he had ever been from home. How would he know the right way to go?

Everything was strange and new. The woods were full of all sorts of enemies. He hoped he would find some friends too.

Fergus found a path above the river and he trotted along, his nose to the ground. His nose could tell him a thousand things. He was trotting along so fast that he bumped into a very strange thing.

Ouch! He hurt his poor nose.

Fergus whimpered. Whatever this thing was, it was very sharp and it was in his way. Fergus backed away from its jagged spikes. He certainly didn't want to play with this animal!

Most of all, he wanted to get back on his adventure.

Soon the sky grew dark and the hills began to disappear. Night had come.

Fergus's paws were cold and he felt tired, but there was no safe place to sleep. Not like the cosy holt he had left behind. He thought of his mother and brothers there, and for a moment he wished he was with them.

But he was on his own, on his journey, and he had to keep going.

Fergus began to hear a strange noise ahead, a kind of roaring. What if it was some awful creature that wanted to eat him?

But this noise was different. It went on and on, louder and louder, until even the ground under the otter's paws was shaking.

Fergus forced himself on through the shadows.

It was just beginning to grow light when Fergus found himself on the edge of a great rock. A waterfall like a horse's tail splashed down into the biggest pool he had ever seen. It was the waterfall that had been roaring!

As the dawn began and it grew brighter and brighter, Fergus saw that this was a special place, with everything an otter could want. Fergus caught sight of something in the bank, a dark shadow that looked familiar. He climbed down to look more closely – for all otters are curious.

And he was right. It was an otter's
holt, very like the one he had left behind.
  Just then, something, or rather
someone, popped their furry head
out of the hole in the bank.

It was another otter. It was Freya. And she had been looking for a new home too.

The young otters stood nose to nose, each just as surprised as the other.

Then Freya scampered down from the holt into the pool.

Fergus, tired as he was, followed her.

The two otters chased about the pool, faster and faster, swimming down right to the bottom and curving round each other in one single otter knot.

Fergus felt happy, so very happy. It had taken him a long time but he had found his new home at last, and a friend.

Picture Kelpies is an imprint of Floris Books
First published in 2010 by Floris Books
Third printing 2013
Text © 2010 Kenneth Steven
Illustrations © 2010 Louise Crowe

Kenneth Steven and Louise Crowe have asserted their right under the
Copyright, Designs and Patent Act 1988 to be identified as the Author and
Illustrator of this Work.

The publisher acknowledges subsidy from Creative Scotland
towards the publication of this volume.

British Library CIP Data available
ISBN 978-086315-778-3

Printed in Singapore